Take Us to Your Sugar

Read more about Beep and Bob's adventures in space!

Take Us to Your Sugar

written and illustrated by Jonathan Roth

ALADDIN

New York   London   Toronto   Sydney   New Delhi

ALADDIN

An imprint of Simon & Schuster Children's Publishing Division
1230 Avenue of the Americas, New York, New York 10020
First Aladdin hardcover edition September 2018
Copyright © 2018 by Jonathan Roth
Also available in an Aladdin paperback edition.
All rights reserved, including the right of reproduction in whole or in part in any form.
ALADDIN and related logo are registered trademarks of Simon & Schuster, Inc.
For information about special discounts for bulk purchases, please contact
Simon & Schuster Special Sales at 1-866-506-1949 or business@simonandschuster.com.
The Simon & Schuster Speakers Bureau can bring authors to your live event. For more information or to book an event contact the Simon & Schuster Speakers Bureau at 1-866-248-3049 or visit our website at www.simonspeakers.com.
Book designed by Nina Simoneaux
The illustrations for this book were rendered digitally.
The text of this book was set in Adobe Caslon Pro.
Manufactured in the United States of America 0818 FFG
2 4 6 8 10 9 7 5 3 1
Library of Congress Control Number 2018930169
ISBN 978-1-4814-8859-4 (hc)
ISBN 978-1-4814-8858-7 (pbk)
ISBN 978-1-4814-8860-0 (eBook)

For Elizabeth and Catherine

★ CONTENTS ★

SPLOG ENTRY #1:
Send Snacks!

Dear Kids of the Past,

Hi. My name's Bob and I live and go to school in space. That's right, space. Pretty sporky, huh? Only a hundred Earth kids are picked to go to Astro Elementary each year, and I was one of them. There's just one micro little problem:

THE FOOD!

I mean, they have the technology to make anything, but the only pizza toppings in our cafeteria are broccoli bits and proton sprinkles!

Beep just said, "Sprinkles, yum!" Beep is a young alien who got separated from his 600 siblings when they were playing hide-and-seek in some asteroid field. Then he floated around space for a while, until he ended up here. Sad, huh?

You know what's even sadder? I was the one who found him knocking on our space station's air lock door and let him in. Now he thinks I'm his new mother! Obviously, Beep can be very confused (especially about food, since he *tastes* with his eyes). But I still like him.

"Beep like Bob-mother, too!"

Beep is pretty good at drawing, so I let him do all the pictures for these space logs (splogs, as we call them). Unfortunately, his pencils are yellow, so he thinks they taste like banana. It's not even snack time, and he's already gone through a dozen!

Anyway, that's my life. Enjoy!

SPLOG ENTRY #2:
A Broken Part

I probably shouldn't have spent so much of the last entry talking about food, because now all I can think about is lunch. To make things worse, Professor Zoome has been telling us about a planet covered with volcanoes that spew hot fudge.

"I'd give anything for some hot fudge," I whispered to Beep. "Anything!"

Beep pouted. "Even give Beep?"

"No, not you, Beep."

He smiled.

"I mean, unless," I added, "it was a whole *lot* of hot fudge."

Lani turned from the seat next to me. Lani, short for Laniakea Supercluster, is supersmart, supercool, and superfun (and possibly super*cute*, not that I notice that kind of thing). "Beep is worth way more than hot fudge," she said. "Even if you poured it on the biggest banana split on Saturn."

"Oooh, banana," Beep said, and gulped down the last of his pencils.

When the lunch

★ 5 ★

bell finally rang, we all shot out of there. "About time," I said. "I'm famished."

"Even after that huge stack of fiberjacks they gave us for breakfast?" Lani asked.

"I only ate the syrup."

Lani made a face. "What about last night's protein patties?"

"I only licked the ketchup."

"Do you eat anything, Bob, that's actually *good* for you?"

"Sure. I had two slices of blueberry cheesecake for dessert." I folded my arms. "Blueberry is fruit."

Beep clapped. "Blueberry, yay!" Blue is one of his favorites.

We floated around a corner and grabbed the railings that led to the cafeteria, which is the one place in our school that has gravity. Gravity is super pricey in space, but it's really hard to keep food on your tray without it. Not to mention chocolate milk.

Mr. Da Vinci, the school's maintenance man, eyed us as we entered. I squirmed uncomfortably. (Okay, so I may have had a major chocolate milk spill recently.)

"Hey, Mr. Da Vinci," I said.

He glared.

"Sorry again about the milk," I said. (Did I mention it was a whole tray? With cartons for my entire class?)

Mr. Da Vinci leaned on his mop and sighed. "All my incredible genius, wasted on the carelessness of children."

I pulled Beep up to the Servo-server. Today's lunch was peanut butter and jelly slabwiches, green matter number B, chocolate milk (no thanks!), and non-astronaut ice cream.

I deleted everything but the jelly and the ice cream.

"I'm allergic to peanuts!" I said to Lani when she shot me a look.

The Servo-server made some cranking sounds and then squirted my order onto my tray. I was particularly excited about *non*-astronaut ice cream for a change. It wasn't even dry and powdery!

Beep waddled next to me. (When he walks, he looks like a penguin.) "Where Beep and Bob-mother sit?" he asked.

This was always tricky. Astro Elementary is full of cliques. The Kids Who Love Math. The Kids Who Really, Really Love Math. The Kids Who Want to Marry Math. And so on.

Me, I'm more of a Kid Who Loves Naps. I like to sit in the back, where you can lean against the wall.

"There," I said, pointing to a table at the far end of the room. "Quick, while it's empty." If I spread out enough, I could even lie down. And no offense to Beep, but he makes a pretty good cushion.

Beep eyed his peanut butter slabwich, then tossed it into his mouth whole.

"You should chew," I said.

"Chew gross," he said.

I put a dab of jelly on my ice cream. "Nothing gross about this. Watch me savor every last drop of goodness."

I shoved a large spoonful into my mouth. "Mmm, mmm," I began to hum, but then I made a very startling and horrific discovery: The ice cream tasted . . . *bad*.

While my throat was already saying, *Swallow*, my brain was saying, *Don't!* With one hack, a stream of jelly and cream spewed out of my nose.

Beep shook his head. "Bob-mother *super* gross."

Of course it was at just that moment that Lani, accompanied by her friend Zenith, chose to join us. Zenith's butt never even hit the seat. "There goes my appetite for a week," she muttered, and spun to leave.

"Bob!" Lani said.

I grabbed a handful of napkins. "It's not"—I hacked again—"not my fault! It's the ice cream and jelly. They're"—I shuddered at the horror—"*not sweet!*"

She took a taste from her own tray. "Blech, you're right. Something must be broken."

A quick glance at the sparks coming off the Servo-server confirmed it. I rushed to Mr. Da Vinci. "There's an emergency! You have to do something! Quick!"

His eyes lit up. "Do you need me to build a device that can control every atom within all six trillion overlapping universes? Because, happily, I'm nearly finished with one!"

There were six trillion universes? "Uh, actually, the Servo-server is on the fritz."

He sighed. "Let me get my tools." He opened the machine and removed a blackened part. "And here we find the problem. The artificial sweetenizer is kaput!"

I froze. In space, it can be very bad when things break. Such as when you're floating in the void, and your oxygen tank gets pierced by a micro-meteor. Or when you're getting ready for bed, and your hyper-toothbrush leaks nuclear plasma.

But none of that comes close to the horror of losing the artificial sweetenizer! *Sweet was my life!* My hands were already shaking from withdrawal.

I grabbed his sleeve. "Tell me you can fix it!"

"Of course I can fix it." He stroked his bushy white beard. "Just have to tinker a bit."

"Will it be done by dinner?!"

"Not a problem, young man. I do my best work in the afternoon."

I let out a sigh. "I guess I can wait that long."

"I'm certain I'll have it by two, maybe three o'clock at the latest." He nodded. "Yes, three o'clock. Of the first Thursday next May."

SPLOG ENTRY #3:
Scream for No Ice Cream

They say in space, no one can hear you scream. But I think that applies only to *outdoor* space, which is a soundless vacuum.

I collapsed onto our lunch table. "Did you hear him, Beep? This is unthinkable. Everything will be unsweetened until next *May*!"

Beep put his arm on my back. "Not so bad, Bob-mother."

"Easy for you to say. As long as your food is colorful, you're fine. But what about me? Do you know how many days it is to next May?" I began to count on my fingers. Tomorrow was September 30, minus the leap year, carry the Tuesday. "Nine thousand!" I said.

Lani rolled her eyes. "Two hundred and fourteen days until Thursday, May first," she said. She was definitely the math-marrying kind.

"When it comes to going without sugar," I admitted, "I'm not sure I can even last another two hundred and fourteen *minutes*."

"Relax, Bob," Lani said. "It could be worse."

"Oh yeah. How?"

"Well, um"—she thought for a moment and then lifted a finger—"the sun could go supernova." Supernovas are when stars collapse into themselves and then explode, vaporizing everything.

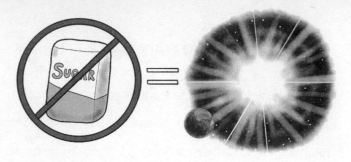

I slumped. "About the same."

"Don't worry," she said. "There's always another solution."

I brightened. "Like asking Principal Quark for a new sweetenizer?"

Lani shuddered. "The last kid who asked the principal for something is still cleaning the plumbing tubes on the outside of the station."

I held up my trembling hands. "See, this is why I always hid a big bag of trick-or-treat candy under my bed back on Earth. For emergencies just like . . . Wait. That's it! Halloween is only"—I calculated on my fingers—"four days away!"

"Actually, thirty-one," Lani said.

I really needed a better math tutor.

"What be Halloween?" Beep asked.

"Halloween," I explained, "is a magical time, Beep. When children dress as monsters and go door-to-door collecting giant bagfuls of free candy." I could feel a tear welling up at the thought of it. "It's the most wonderful day of the year."

Beep's eyes widened. "Bob-mother be monster?"

"Just for pretend, Beep. Or I could dress as a ghost. Or an alien."

"Bob-mother already alien."

"No, Beep. *You're* the alien."

"Beep *alien*?!"

I sighed. "We've gone over this."

He began to bounce and flap his arms. "Beep not alien! Beep not alien!"

"Fine, Beep. You're *not* an alien."

"Beep want meet other not alien," he said. "Other Beeps."

"There aren't any other Beeps here."

"No Beeps?" he said, his eyes filling with tears. I quickly tossed him a pencil. He swallowed it whole.

"You better?" I asked.

"Beep better."

"You know what?" I said. "I'm better too. Even though we've been struck by an unspeakable tragedy, I think I can summon the will to survive another month. Then I'll simply collect enough sweets to last for six years, and that should get me through June."

"Uh, Bob?" Lani said. "Remember when I said it could be worse?"

"What?"

"Promise me you won't scream?"

"Yes, yes, I promise."

"Good. Because, as much as you like Halloween, I think you should know that—well, I'm not sure how far it goes back, at least before I started here . . ."

"Just say it!!"

"Bob." She looked into my eyes. "In space, there *is* no Halloween."

Everything went black.

SPLOG ENTRY #4:
Serious Club Arguments
Really End Sadly

I wish I could say I woke to find it had all been a horrible dream. But as my eyes opened upon a circle of kids (and Beep) staring down at me, I knew it was all too real.

"It's okay, everyone," Lani said. "He's alive."

The crowd immediately lost interest and backed away. Lani held out her hand. "Do you need to go to the nurse?"

I flinched at the mention of Nurse Lance. "No, no! I'm fine. I'm not even seeing little yellow flashing spots on the ceiling."

Lani looked up. "But there *are* little yellow flashing spots on the ceiling."

I squinted. "Really?"

She helped me to my seat. "You don't have to go to the nurse if you promise not to faint again."

"I promise."

"Good. Because, as I was saying, you can't count on Halloween to solve your sugar problems, because we don't celebrate it here."

"GAAAAHHHHHHHHHHH!"

"Bob, you promised you wouldn't scream!"

"Okay, okay. So why can't we have Halloween?"

"Principal Quark has a strict policy against celebrating *any* planetary-based holidays."

★ 21 ★

"But that's no fair! There must be something we can do."

"Well," Lani said, "we can always gather a group of students and come up with a reasonable list of demands."

"I meant, like time travel."

"I like my plan better," she said.

No one ever likes time travel.

Lani leaned in close. "We should act fast. Gather some kids who believe in the cause and meet me in my room after school."

"But I like to nap after school."

"Bob, do you want to take back Halloween or what?"

I raised a fist. "Or what!"

"Great, you're in charge of snacks. See you there!"

« * « ★ » * »

At exactly 3:05, Beep and I knocked on Lani's dorm room door. I wasn't crazy about missing a nap, but without my normal sugar crash, I actually wasn't all that tired.

She peered down the hall, then let us in. "Bob, I told you to bring others."

"I brought Beep."

"Okay, then, Beep," she said, "who did *you* bring?"

"Beep bring Flash," he said.

"I don't see Flash."

"Beep lose Flash," he said with a pout.

"How can you *lose* Flash?"

Beep shrugged. "Happen fast."

"Well, at least I got Zenith and Hadron to come," Lani said. "Hope that will be enough."

We floated into a circle. Lani raised a small gavel. "I hereby begin the first meeting of the secret club known as S.C.A.R.E.S."

"S.C.A.R.E.S.?" I asked.

Lani smiled. "It's a clever acronym I came up with: Scary Costumes Are the Right of Every Student!"

Beep backed away. "Beep no like scary."

"But it's about Halloween," Lani said.

"I thought it was about free treats," I said, then thought for a second. "Maybe S.C.A.R.E.S. should stand for the Society of Candy Addicts who Rely on Energy from Sugar."

"Good one, Bob," Hadron said, and we high-fived.

"As the president and founder of S.C.A.R.E.S., I say this is not up for discussion!" Lani said. "We're

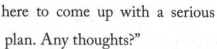

here to come up with a serious plan. Any thoughts?"

Beep waved. "Beep president too?"

"There's only one president,"

Lani said. Beep pouted. "Fine, you can be *vice* president, Beep."

Zenith gasped. "Hey, you said *I* could be vice president!"

"I said I'd *think* about it," Lani said.

"Well, then I *think* I'm going to leave," Zenith said, and huffed away.

"The vice president has no real power!" Lani called after her.

"Beep power no real?" Beep said.

"Only if I die," Lani said.

Beep clapped. "Yay die!"

"Wait," Hadron said. "Who said anything about *dying*?"

"No one's going to die," Lani said. "The worst thing that's going to happen is that we won't make it out of Principal Quark's office alive."

Hadron spun for the door. "I just remembered. I have chess club on Tuesday."

"Today's Wednesday."

The door swished open. "Bye!"

Lani banged the table with her gavel. "Even though S.C.A.R.E.S. is down to just the three of us, I still think we can do this."

"Uh, do what exactly?" I asked.

"March into Principal Quark's office first thing

in the morning to demand our rights!" She pushed us toward the door. "So you better rest up. You'll need all your strength and more if she decides to punish us. See you both then!"

SPLOG ENTRY #5:
Principal's Principles

Between my fear of Principal Quark and my greater fear of no candy, I hardly slept a wink. I was still in pajamas when I heard a knock at our door the next morning.

"Beep! Bob! Wake up!" Lani called. "Time to go."

"Coming," I groaned, and got dressed.

We floated down the hall. "Have you given

thought to what you're going to say to the principal?"
Lani asked.

"I have to say something?!" I asked.

"Beep give thought," Beep said.

Lani smiled. "That's wonderful, Beep."

"About club secret shake," he said, and held out his
arm. "Go up, up, down, round."

I took hold of his hand
and tried to follow
along. "Up, down,
up, around?"

"Up, *up*, down, round."

"Guys, we're here!" Lani said.

We entered the front office.

"May I help you?" asked Secretary Octoblob.
Secretary Octoblob was one of the few alien staff

members. He/she/it? had eight suction-pad arms, which were always brimming with phones, rosters, charts, staplers, and an occasional student who came too close and couldn't get unstuck.

"We're here to see Principal Quark," Lani said.

"Did you do something bad?" he/she/it? asked.

"No."

"Did you do something *really* bad?" he/she/it? asked.

"No."

"Did you do something really, really, *really*—"

Lani straightened. "We would like to see her about an important proposal. Concerning her policy about holidays."

Secretary Octoblob's eye widened. "Holidays? Proposal? *Now?*"

"Yes, please."

"Oh, this should prove quite interesting. I'll buzz

you right in." As he/she/it? reached for the button, a student caught in an arm broke free.

"Finally!" Flash gasped, shooting away.

"Oh, hey, Flash," I said. So *that's* where he'd been.

Principal Quark's office was down a cold, dark hallway. When we came to the end, a steel door slid to the side. Then another slid up. Then another from the other side. Then a spiky iron gate. Beyond it was dark and misty.

"Uh, maybe we should come back," I said. "Like, in a *thousand* years."

"Just go," Lani said, nudging me forward.

Once inside, our eyes began to adjust to the darkness. Something lurked behind the desk, making a terrible hissing and sputtering sound.

"Principal Quark?" Lani said to the desk. "Is that you?"

"Huh? Wha?" The lights suddenly came on, and Principal Quark's eyes popped open. She blinked a few times. "What's going on?"

Lani cleared her throat. "I think we, um, woke you."

The principal's face reddened. "I was not *asleep*. I was deep in thought. I am a very deep thinker."

I winked. "I like to *think* too."

She looked me over. "It doesn't particularly show. Anyway, now that you're here, and I'm in a foul mood, please tell me what you want."

Lani pushed me forward. "Yes, tell her what we want, Bob."

"Me? But I, uh . . ." I pushed Beep forward. "Yes, tell her what we want, Beep."

"Beep want more Beeps!"

"I mean," I whispered, "tell her the *yummy* you want."

Beep nodded. "Beep want blueberry!"

"Blueberry," Principal Quark said, "is available in the Servo-server."

Beep clapped. "Yay!"

"Oh, aren't you a cute one?" the principal said, smiling.

★ 33 ★

"She likes him," Lani whispered to me. "This is our opening. Do something."

I floated a few inches closer to the principal's desk. "I think what Beep *meant* to say—and please remember how very, very cute he is—is that what we all really want is Halloween."

Principal Quark slammed her hands on her desk. "Out of the question!"

"But why?" I asked.

"Simple, young Bob. If Astro Elementary began celebrating planetary holidays, there would be no end. Every day is a holiday somewhere. Do you really want a party *every single day of the school year*?"

"Definitely!" I said, turning to Lani. This was turning out great!

Lani hissed, "She was speaking *rhetorically*. You weren't supposed to answer."

"But it's Halloween," I said to the principal. "Can't you just make an eensy-weensy exception?"

"I am very firm on rules," she said. "There are no exceptions."

Maybe this wasn't turning out so great.

Lani pulled me aside. "S.C.A.R.E.S. is failing! What are we going to do?"

I shrugged. "Too bad there aren't *space* holidays."

Lani gasped. "That's it. Bob, you're a genius!"

"I am?"

"Well, not in math," she said. "Or in science. Or in any actual subject. But still." She spun to face Principal Quark. "You said we can't have any planetary-based holidays. But what about one that's based in *space*?"

The principal laced her fingers. "Continue."

"Well," Lani said, "there's this really interesting cosmic holiday called, uh . . ." She turned to me.

"Called, uh . . . ," I said.

"Called Astroween," Lani continued. "And, um, Astroween comes this time every year, on the very last . . ."

"Very *first* . . . ," I corrected.

"Yes, sorry, on the very *first* day of October."

"And what, please tell me," Principal Quark said, "does one *do* on Astroween?"

"All sorts of fun things," Lani said. "But mainly, on Astroween, kids dress up as their favorite aliens, to help celebrate the, um . . ."

"To help celebrate the diversity of aliens everywhere!" I said.

Principal Quark held us in her gaze for what felt like an hour. "Interesting," she said.

"Uh, but don't forget, Lani," I said, "to tell the principal about the most *important* part of Astroween."

"What could be more important than celebrating diversity?" Lani said.

"Earth to Lani," I whispered. "The *candy*."

Lani shot me a look. "Yes, I was getting to that part of Astroween where all the kids march from door to door and say . . . What do they say again, Bob?"

I gulped. I couldn't say *trick or treat*, because that was obviously from Halloween. And besides, wasn't it time to retire the trick part anyhow? Let's be honest here, no kid who goes through all the bother of dressing up wants some goofy dad who thinks he knows how to entertain kids coming up with some dorky . . .

"I'm waiting," Principal Quark said.

"Oh, right. Sorry. What they say is"—I glanced over at Beep, who was playing with a sock, and it gave me an idea—"sock or . . . sweet! Because aliens like socks." At least Beep did. "And kids like sweets!"

"See how inclusive it is," Lani said.

"And then people give the kids tons of free candy!" I added. "The end."

Principal Quark pinched her chin. "Hmm. Astroween. Intriguing. I'll have to think about it." She shut her eyes and immediately began to snore.

Lani sighed. "Well, Bob, we tried. But I guess it just isn't meant to—" She jumped as Principal Quark popped awake.

"I have considered your request," she said, "and since it violates no rules, we can give it a try." She picked up her phone. "I'll have my secretary make the arrangements. Anything else, children?"

"No. No, we're good."

"Then you may leave now. Quickly, I suggest, before the spiky iron gate cuts you in two. Have a nice day!"

SPLOG ENTRY #6:
Lanced a Lot

As we passed back through the front office, Secretary Octoblob was already juggling a dozen (well, eight) different Astroween-related preparation tasks.

"One day's notice," he/she/it? said to us. "Thank you, children, for *that*."

Out in the hall, we did somersaults in the air and slapped high fives (in the case of Beep, high *ones*).

"We did it!" Lani said. "We get to wear costumes! And we only had to change the name, date, and complete history of Halloween to do it!"

"Costumes, that's right!" I said. "How are we going to get cool alien costumes by tomorrow?"

"Beep know good alien dress-up," Beep said. He yanked on the frayed end of the sock he was playing with until it was a mess of yarn.

"What's that for?" I dared to ask.

He then bunched the yarn and stuck it on his head. "Me be Bob-mother! Very alien scary. Gaahhhhh!"

This time it was Lani who clapped. "Very good impression, Beep!"

"Okay, okay," I said. "And you can stop doing somersaults now."

Lani looked at me. "We're not doing somersaults."

"Oh. Maybe I'm just dizzy with happiness."

Lani took my hand. "You're trembling again. I think it must be from lack of proper nutrients. Luckily, we're right by the nurse's office."

"Not Nurse Lance!" I said.

Lani yanked me toward the door. "Bob, you're not going to scream now, are you? Like—how does that go again, Beep?"

Beep went, "Gaaahhhhhhh!"

Lani laughed. "Just perfect."
Then she clamped her hand
on my back and, to my horror,
shoved me through the door.
"See ya."

"Well, hello again, Bob," Nurse Lance said to Beep. "What seems to be the problem?"

"That's Beep!" I said.

Nurse Lance studied Beep closely. "Well, so it is. Remarkable resemblance."

"He's wearing an old sock on his head!" I said.

The nurse turned my way. "So, Bob, once again, please tell me, what brought you into this soothing chamber of healing?"

"Well, I guess it all began when—"

"Yes, that's quite enough," Nurse Lance said. "We'll just strap you in the cold, hard chair and stuff you full of medicine."

"No, wait, I . . . hey, that really *is* cold."

He put his stethoscope on my forehead. "Hmm, heartbeat very faint."

"That's my head!"

"Say *ahhh*."

"Ahhh."

He looked into my mouth and made a face. "Well,

there's the main problem. You have a gross dangly thing in the back of your throat."

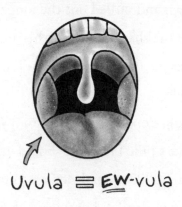

Uvula ≡ <u>EW</u>-vula

"That's always been there."

"Still, I should probably cut it out."

"What? No! My problem is sugar! The sweetenizer broke, and I don't have any hidden candy, and I'm just faint from it all! Please don't cut anything! Please!"

Nurse Lance nodded. "Ah, a simple sucrose imbalance. Why didn't you just say so?"

"Well, I tried to, but—"

"Fortunately for you, I have just the solution." He reached down and pulled out the longest needle I've ever seen! "One sharp jab from this and—"

"No, please, GAHHHHH! There must be another way!"

The needle stopped, inches from my neck. "Well, you *could* take a pill. Though I should inform you that it will take 0.00002 seconds longer to take effect."

"That's fine! Really! Anything but the shot. Anything!"

With a sigh, he put the needle away and unstrapped me. I felt a million times better already. "So," I said. "Where's my pill?"

He gestured to the medicine cabinet. "Take your pick. They all have sugar in them."

"They do?" I floated closer to inspect the selection.

"Of course they do. They're for children."

"But"—and I can't believe I was about to say this—"isn't sugar *bad* for you?"

He shrugged. "Eh."

I reached for a bottle that said TOOTHACHE MEDICINE. I had been having a little of that anyway. "What's the right dose? Will too much harm me?"

"Not at all. You see, once all the sweeteners are crammed into those pills, they have zero real medicine left."

"You mean, all this time . . . all this sugar . . . right *here*?"

He nodded. "Hope it helps, Bob."

I floated toward the door. "I'm sure it will, Nurse Lance. I'm sure it will."

SPLOG ENTRY #7:
Cosmic Costuming

After enjoying a dose or three of my new "medicine," I floated back into Professor Zoome's classroom, where everyone was already talking about the new space holiday.

I went up to Lani. "Who did you tell?"

"Only Zenith," she said.

Who obviously then told Andromeda. Who told

Flash. Who told Blaster. Who told Comet. Who told Hadron. Who told . . .

"Bob-mother!" Beep said. "Tomorrow Astroween!" Beep put the "Bob" wig on. "Sock or sweet!"

"Attention, class!" Professor Zoome yelled.

Everyone landed in their seats.

"No, not you, Bob," she said. "I need you up front."

Gulp.

"Bob," she said, "I know there's a lot of excitement about this rather suddenly announced holiday you told Principal Quark about called Astroween."

Double gulp.

"In fact, I've been researching it everywhere, and I can't find a single reference at all."

Triple gulp.

"And so, Bob, I need you to be completely honest with me about something."

What comes after triple gulp? Fourple? Purple? Vermilion?

"Yes, Professor Zoome?"

She pulled a bottle out of her desk. "What I need to know is: Should I put glittery blue streaks in my hair to dress up as one of the sixty queens of Venus? Or should I encase my head in a large brain to represent the telepaths of Einsteinium-7?"

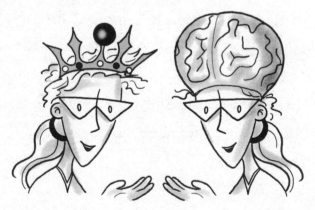

I shuddered at both thoughts. But at least I wasn't busted.

"I think in the time-honored spirit of Astroween . . . ," I began.

"Yes?" she asked.

"You should do what you think is best."

Before she could respond, Beep swooped down and grabbed her bottle. "Blue glittery, yum!" And then it was gone.

"The big brain thing sounds cool," I said. "A definite Astroween winner."

"Then that is what I shall be." She turned to the class. "Well, what are you waiting for? We have but one day to prepare. Class dismissed!"

As Beep, Lani, and I floated down the halls, classroom doors swished open all around us. Word had spread fast. The entire school was in full Astroween prep mode.

"This is great," I said. "We should make up a new holiday every day. Especially now that my 'medicine' is gone." I tossed the empty bottle.

Lani caught the floating bottle and stuffed it in her pocket. "No excuse to litter." She then turned a corner. "Quick. We need costumes. And I know just the place."

"Me too," I said. "Astrozon Prime will ship overnight to anywhere in the solar system. And it only costs a sideways 8!"

"That's infinity, Bob."

"Oh." I was glad I wouldn't be home when Mom got the bill for those socks I had overnighted after Beep ate my last pair. "So where *are* we going to order our costumes?"

"Silly Bob. We're not going to *buy* our costumes." She slowed in front of the art room, and I had a very bad feeling about what she was going to say next. "We're going to make them!"

Okay, it's embarrassing to admit, but art is probably my worst subject (not including math, science, reading, music, and PE). The waxy feel of crayons gives me the jitters. And I still have nightmares about that time I got a glob of papier-mâché down my shirt.

"Create time, yay!" Beep said. He, of course, is amazing at drawing. Plus, he loves to eat blue paint.

"C'mon. It'll be fun," Lani said, pulling me inside.

The art room was already packed with desperate kids who also must have maxed out their parents' bank accounts. Ms. Splatz, the art teacher, turned to greet us.

She smiled. "Hi, Beep. Hello, Lani." Her smile faded. "Bob."

Okay, so last week I may have spilled a large can of brown paint. Sue me already.

"We're here to make costumes," Lani said.

"You and half the school! It's wonderful. I've set up paint in that area, beads and feathers in that one, tentacles and pipe cleaner antennae right there, and for those of you who *aren't* afraid of papier-mâché, a station in the back."

I cringed at the sight of big blobs of papier-mâché floating next to strips of torn newspaper. (Newspapers were how people got their news back in prehistoric times on Earth.)

"Let's go to the painting station," Lani said. Sadly, the paint was bobbing around in little globules too, mixing with the feathers and beads. The school should

probably splurge on gravity for the art room, too.

Lani grabbed a brush. "I'm going to make a costume in the style of the indigenous large blue people of Pandemonium. What about you, Bob?" Lani asked.

"What kind of alien species are you going to be?"

"Let me think. Which kind have the coolest laser blasters?"

"You can't have laser blasters with your costume! But you can choose something else." She grabbed some fluffy feathers.

"No way," I said.

"How about these tentacle things?"

I picked one up. It was squishy, sticky, and gross. "Double no way." But as I was putting it down, I noticed that some beads and other stuff were already stuck to it.

And then, possibly for the first time ever, I had a pretty good idea.

SPLOG ENTRY #8:
Bob-Monster

Okay, so maybe lugging eight tentacle-thingies back to my room wasn't the easiest task, but I knew it was going to be well worth it. After Lani and Beep helped me, I told them my plan.

"It's very nice, Bob," Lani said, "that you're going to be celebrating the species of Secretary Octoblob. I'm sure he/she/it? will appreciate it."

"Yeah, and think how many candy bags I'll be able to carry with all these! Eight arms times about ten suction cups on each arm times fifty pieces of candy in each bag equals"—I calculated with all my might—"two thousand yummy treats!"

"Four thousand," Lani said.

"Yes, but I always eat half before I get home."

Beep clapped. "Bob-mother candy math good!"

I shrugged. "Numbers have *some* uses."

I peeled a tentacle that was stuck to my back. "These things sure are hard to use. Maybe I don't need so many."

Lani sighed. "But then you wouldn't be honoring Secretary Octoblob. And it's such a nice gesture, considering how lonely he/she/it? must feel."

"Why would Secretary Octoblob feel lonely?" I said.

Lani leaned in and whispered, "You'd be lonely

too, if you were the only one of your species around."

I pointed at Beep. "Beep is the only one of his species around, and he's okay." I slapped him on the back. "Aren't you, buddy?"

But Beep was suddenly not looking so okay. "Beep try hard forget." His big eyes welled up. "But now Bob-mother remind."

Lani glared at me. "Now look what you did."

"Beep sad!"

Lani leaned to hug him. "There, there, Beep. Just because Bob is an insensitive monster, doesn't mean you have to cry."

"Hey, what did I do?"

Lani grabbed a box of tissues. "Here, Beep. Use these."

Beep gulped the blue box down. "Lani-friend nice."

"I'm nice too," I said. "Remember, I'm the one

who lets you call me 'mother,' even though I'm clearly not."

Beep's eyes got teary again. "Bob-mother not Beep mother?"

Lani kicked me. "Of *course* he's your mother. Isn't that right, *Bob*?"

I gritted my teeth. "Yes, Beep. I'm your new mother. Are we all happy now?"

Beep clapped. "Beep say yay!"

Lani put her hand on Beep. "Nothing's more important than family and friends, Beep."

"Especially on Astroween," I added.

"Beep wish more Beeps come for sock or sweet," Beep said. "Bob-mother bring?"

I wasn't about to break it to him that even if I knew where to find his home planet, I doubted one of his siblings would make an intergalactic trip for a made-up holiday. But I felt I owed him, so I said, "I'll tell you what, Beep. I'll send out an invitation. Just promise me you won't get your hopes up."

Beep bounced. "Hopes up! Hopes up!"

I went to my computer and opened Spacebook, which is how we post random messages out to space. "What should we say?"

Beep thought for a moment. "Hmm . . ."

"Make it honest," Lani said. "Sweet, but not too sappy. Simple, but not too—"

"CANDY FREE COME! CANDY FREE COME!" Beep said.

I typed that in and hit enter.

"And now that that's done, let's get ready," I said. "Because no matter what happens, one thing's for sure: Tomorrow is going to be the best Astroween ever!"

SPLOG ENTRY #9:
Beep Bag

I woke in my dorm room extremely relaxed and refreshed. I stretched my arms and knocked on the bunk above. "Beep, you awake?"

He peeked down. "Beep wake. Bob-mother wake?"

"You can *see* I'm awake, Beep. In fact, it was the best night's sleep I've had in ages. Probably because I slept so bad the night before." I floated out from the covers. "At least it's still early. It would have been a nightmare to oversleep on Astroween."

"No early," Beep said. "Past lunch."

"It's not past lunch, Beep. Look." I pointed at the starry night out the window. And then I remembered it was always like that!

Beep held up the bedside clock. "See. Day."

"*One thirty!* Oh no! Beep, why did you let me sleep so long?!"

"Bob-mother like sleep."

"Yes, but not *today!*"

"Plus, Bob-mother cute when sleep."

"Quick, we have to get in costume!" When Beep put his "Bob" wig on, I added, "I mean, me. Help *me* get all these awful tentacles on."

It wasn't easy. Every time I got one attached, it would stick to others. Before I knew it, all the tentacles were balled in a slithery, sticky mess.

"This is useless!" I kicked at the tentacles, and they suctioned off my shoe. Finally, I settled for wearing one. "There. Do I look like an alien?"

"Bob-mother always look alien."

That was good enough for me. I faced the door. "Then what are we waiting for?"

"For Bob-mother brush teeth?"

"Sheesh, Beep, who has time for that? Let's go!"

To my horror the Astroween activities were already in full swing at school. I pushed through the crowded hall.

"Bob, Beep, there you are!" Lani called. "I've been

looking for you everywhere." I turned toward her voice and saw a sleek purple girl with big ears and a tail.

"Wow, is that you?" I said. "Your costume looks so real."

She smiled. "Thanks. Took me about three hours to apply the paint alone." She glanced at the one limp tentacle sticking out of my chest. "What happened to the other seven?"

"Long story."

"But you were supposed to dress as an *actual* alien species."

"Hey, I tried!" I said. "So, what have I missed?"

"The costume parade, zero-grav apple bobbing, an Earth bounce, pin the antenna on the space donkey, bag decorating . . ."

"The candy! Have I missed any candy?!"

She held up her bag (decorated with glitter, felt stars, glitter, googly eyes, math equations, and more glitter). "Just started. Grab a bag and join me!"

"Will do!" I looked around. "Where are the bags, anyway? I'll need about ten."

She led me toward the bag decorating station. "Uh-oh. Looks like they're all gone. See what happens when you sleep in?!"

"There must be something I can use." A backpack

or pillowcase would do, but those were both back in my room. I glanced around. At Beep. At the empty table. At Lani. And then back at Beep.

"Beep, little buddy! How much can your pouch tummy hold?"

He spread his arms. "Beep hold lot and lot more!"

"Perfect!" I said. "Beep, will you be our Astroween candy bag?"

"Beep bag! Beep bag!"

"Great," I said. "Let's fill you up!"

SPLOG ENTRY #10:
Ding, Dong

have to say, the next hour was one of the best of my life. There we were, three friends on an October school day, going from classroom to classroom and saying, "Sock or sweet!" Teachers opened their doors and poured all sorts of yummy candies into our bags (or, in my case, into Beep). It was glorious.

"C'mon, Beep, what are you waiting for?" I said as

he stopped to look out a window. "We have two more floors to go."

He kept his eyes on the stars. "When more Beeps come?"

"I told him not to get his hopes up," I whispered to Lani.

"I feel terrible," she said.

"Then eat some candy."

She looked in her bag, then wrinkled her nose with disgust. "I don't even *like* candy."

I shuddered. "Do I even know you?!"

"Well, mint gum, maybe," she said. "I haven't had any of that since leaving Earth. But all this—"

Beep interrupted with a happy cry, and "Beeps come! Beeps come!"

I turned. "What?"

He pointed out the window at an approaching fleet of small ships. "Beeps come for Astroween! Beep go let in." Then he took off.

"Wait for us, Beep! You don't know who they are!"

But Beep was fast. By the time we caught up to him at the air lock, the first ship was already docking. It clanked into place and whooshed steam. (Space sounds are cool.)

The air lock bell then chimed *ding, dong, ding.* (Okay, not all space sounds.)

I peered out the portal. "I can't see anyone. They're too short."

"Like Beeps! Like Beeps!"

"Maybe," I said, "but school rules say that we're really not supposed to let anyone in until . . ."

Beep hit the button and the door slid open. (He's never been one for school rules.)

And before I could say hello, I found myself in the clutches of a long, slithering tentacle.

SPLOG ENTRY #11:
Sugar Blues

The good news is, I didn't die. You can tell I didn't die because I'm still writing my splog. FYI, a sudden STOP in my splog = bad news.

But even though I didn't die, it wasn't exactly pleasant being gripped by a long, slimy tentacle. Especially because the tentacle pulled my face close to the extremely slimy and ugly (let's call it slugly) face of an alien.

"M-may I help you?" I said.

"Take. Us. To. Your. Sugar!" it demanded.

"S-sugar?"

Lani, off to the side, said, "I think it means leader. Take us to your *leader*."

"I mean *sugar*!" the alien said, squeezing me harder.

"Here!" Lani said, holding out her bag. "Take all the candy you want."

"Oooh," the alien said, and tossed me aside. He looked in the bag, then handed it to another one like him. For the first time, I noticed they all had only one tentacle each, coming out of their chests.

"Hey, I'm dressed as one of you." I turned to Lani. "See!"

"To mimic our kind is an insult worthy of death!" the alien said.

I yanked the tentacle off and chucked it. "Not mimicking! Not mimicking!"

I'm still writing my splog, so you can see my plan worked.

The alien with the candy bag said, "This is not nearly enough. We need more."

Lani leaned in to whisper, "Whatever we do, Bob, we better not tell them about Astroween."

"I'm not going to tell them about Astroween." I turned. "Are you, Beep?"

"Beep no tell Astroween." He turned to one of the aliens. "You tell Astroween?"

"Not me," the alien said. Then: "Wait, what is Astroween?"

The chief alien, who I'll just call Sluglyface, said, "Do not try to deceive us. We received your invitation. CANDY FREE COME, it said."

"Good going, Bob," Lani muttered.

"Hey, you were there too!"

Sluglyface turned to his forces. "Search the entire station. Take every morsel you find!"

"Wait. *Every* morsel?" I said.

"Looks like you're not the only one with a sweet tooth, Bob," Lani said.

Sluglyface gasped. "You *eat* the candy?"

"Uh, you don't?"

"Sugar is the fuel we use to run our fleet," he said. "To eat such a poison is un*thinkable*."

Suddenly more and more aliens poured through

the door. Soon the school was going to be swarming with them. Unless I thought of something. And fast.

"It's too bad there's not an emergency intercom on the wall," I said to Lani. "Then we could warn everyone."

"But there *is* an emergency intercom on the wall." She pointed. "Right behind that big alien guard."

I shrugged. "Well, so much for that idea."

"Bob, don't be so gutless! All I have to do is distract him."

"Wait, Lani . . . !"

But she had already floated up to the guard. "Oops, silly me," she said. "I seem to have lost a gumdrop."

"Hmm, must find it," the guard said, and bent to look.

"NOW, BOB! GO!"

Before I could talk myself out of it, I shot toward

the intercom and hit the red button. It crackled to life.

"Attention, everyone!" I said. "Astro Elementary has been invaded by candy-stealing aliens! Anyone who looks like a candy-hungry alien is an invader! Hide all your candy and fight for your lives!" A tentacle then covered my mouth, and I found myself being tossed back toward Lani.

I brushed my hands together. "Well, that was pretty amazing of me, I must say."

"Bob," she said. "You dolt! Today *everyone* looks like a candy-hungry alien!"

SPLOG ENTRY #12:
We're Goo

Okay, so my poor choice of words may have started a mass panic. What can you do?

As if things couldn't get worse, some more of the aliens then pushed some kind of contraption through the door. It had a big opening at the top and a spout at the bottom.

"What's that?" I asked.

Sluglyface put his hand on it and grinned. "This is the Gooifier."

"And what does a"—gulp—"Gooifier do?"

Sluglyface leaned so close, I could smell his slugly breath. "It *gooifies*." He then took Lani's bag of candy and tossed it inside.

"NO!" I said, but I was too late. The Gooifier made chopping, gurgling, and popping sounds (Gooifier sounds are cool too.) And then: plop. Goo came out of the spout.

Sluglyface held up a full jar. "Behold: perfectly pure rocket fuel."

Or perfectly pure candy syrup. "I don't suppose I could, uh, taste it?" I asked.

Sluglyface grimaced, then turned to his soldiers. "Now take the Gooifier to the dining hall. And bring the prisoners!"

Minutes later we were roughly herded into the cafeteria. And not just us: lots of dazed-looking kids, teachers, and even Principal Quark (who looked like she had been woken from some very deep "thinking" time).

But even worse, right in the middle of the room was every candy bag in the school. They were going to gooify it all!

I couldn't help but shudder as bag after bag was tossed inside and chopped, gurgled, popped, and plopped into goo. At least I still had *my* candy safely hidden inside Beep. When every crumb was gone, Sluglyface counted the jars. "This is not enough. We need one more to power our fleet!"

Principal Quark stepped forward. "You've taken it all. Now go."

"There must be a bag we overlooked!" Sluglyface said.

Next to me, Beep began to say, "Beep bag! Beep b—"

I clamped his mouth. "Beep, shhh!"

But it was too late: Sluglyface had heard. He approached Beep. "You dare to conceal candy from us?"

Beep patted his tummy. "Beep bag for Bob-mother."

Sluglyface's eyes gleamed. "You heard him. Throw the little alien in!"

"Who alien?" Beep said.

"You are *all* aliens," Sluglyface said.

"Beep no alien! You alien!"

"Since when are *we* aliens?" Sluglyface said.

"Since born."

"Pah, this is pointless. Throw him in now!"

I jumped forward. "No! You can't!"

"And *you* can't stop us!"

That was probably true. Not by fighting, anyway. But how, then? As they took Beep away, they held us all back.

"Bob, we have to do something!" Lani said.

"Like?"

She slipped away and ran.

But can I blame her? After all, it wasn't Lani's fault we had gotten into this mess. (Actually, it was

Mr. Da Vinci's; if only he had fixed the sweetenizer when it first broke, then we never would have had to make up a new holiday that somehow led to this hostile invasion.)

And yet, in a small way, it was my fault too. So before I could talk myself out of it, I pulled free and said, "Wait, no! Take *me* instead."

Sluglyface chuckled. "But you are not a candy bag."

"Listen, mister," I said. "I've been eating nothing but sugared cereal, syrup, jelly, soda, and caramels since I was old enough to open a refrigerator. And that's just for breakfast! The truth is, I'm probably more sugar than boy. Not that I'm proud of it, and if I somehow survive this, I vow to eat *healthy* from now on, but for now I—"

"Enough already," Sluglyface said. "Throw them *both* in."

TAKE US TO YOUR SUGAR

"GAHHHHH!" I screamed as a tentacle swooped me up and held me directly over the machine.

Which I know sounds bad, but as long as you're still reading this, it means I . . .

SPLOG ENTRY #13:
Sweet Surprise

Oops, sorry about that. Just dropped my splog-o-matic recording tablet. Right at the exciting part too.

Anyway, as I was saying, as long as you're still reading this, it means I didn't get turned into goo! (Beep didn't, either, in case you were wondering.) I mean, sure, it seemed touch and go for a minute there, but just as my head was dangling over the little choppers, I heard the cafeteria door swish open, and a voice yelled, "HERE! HERE'S ALL YOU NEED AND MORE!"

I pulled myself up just in time to see . . . Lani! Carrying an overflowing bag! While I assumed she had run away for good, she had really broken free and found some more sweets. But where?

To answer, Nurse Lance darted up behind her, screaming, "NOOOOOOOO! That's the school's entire supply!"

"It's one hundred percent sweetener," Lani said. "Does the medicine even work?"

"No," he admitted. "But at least children take it."

He *did* have a point.

Sluglyface swiped the bag away. "This will do nicely. Let those two go."

Beep and I broke free of the tentacles and shot away.

"Yay Lani!" Beep said.

After they had all the fuel they needed, the aliens began to pack up.

"And now we will leave," Sluglyface said, "and not return until this very day next year and on every day you call Astroween from now on in order to replenish our supplies."

Oh, great, just what we needed. A yearly shake-down. But just as I was about to give up hope of ever eating candy again, Mr. Da Vinci stepped forward to study the Gooifier.

"Interesting," he said. "Looks like you don't need sugar at all for your fuel."

"We don't?" Sluglyface said.

Mr. Da Vinci bent down. "See this switch here? You have

it set to SUGAR. But with one little flick . . . there. Now it's set to SALT."

"But how will that help us?"

"Well, for starters, the dried ocean beds of Hydrocon-Six have more salt for the taking than you could use in a million years."

"My sister-in-law lives on Hydrocon-Six!" Sluglyface said. "This is most welcome news."

Mr. Da Vinci shrugged. "I do what I can."

"You are a genius," Sluglyface said. "Perhaps you would consider joining us on our journeys."

"What, and leave all these children I have come to know so well?" Mr. Da Vinci said. He then threw down his mop. "Finally, someone who appreciates me! Ciao, kids, ciao!"

And so they finished packing and left, never to bother us again (???????).

《 * 《 ✪ 》 * 》

Afterward, I stood with Beep and Lani in the empty cafeteria.

"So how did you know about the medicine?" I asked Lani.

"Before I recycled the bottle you tossed, I read the ingredients on the side."

"At least it all ended happily," I said.

"It did?"

"Sure. The aliens got their fuel. Mr. Da Vinci got a new job away from milk-spilling kids. And I"—I patted Beep—"still have some candy."

"But, Bob," Lani said. "You vowed to eat *healthy* from now on if you survived."

"Hey, you were at the nurse's office when I said that."

"Actually, I was waiting right outside the door when you made your little speech."

"Waiting for what? They were about to kill me!"

"I know," she said, smiling. "Which means my dramatic timing was perfect!"

I folded my arms. "Okay. Well, at least everyone *else* is happy."

Lani nodded toward Beep. "Not everyone, Bob."

"Beep?" I said to him.

Beep sniffed. "More Beeps no come after all."

"Oh, Beep, it'll be okay." I looked at Lani. "Won't it?"

She gave me a look that said I better make this right.

"Um, I just remembered," I said, "there's something I have to do. Lani, how about you bring Beep to Professor Zoome's classroom in about twenty minutes?"

I then flew out of the cafeteria and down to the art room. I quickly cut a bunch of construction paper and made it back to Professor Zoome's just ahead of Lani and Beep. I hovered in front of the door as they tried to come in.

"Before you come in, Beep," I said, "shut your eyes."

"Then Beep no see."

"It's a surprise."

"Oooh, Beep like surprise!"

Lani led him to the center of the room, and the entire class surrounded him.

"You can open your eyes now."

Beep's eyes widened as he saw that each one of us was wearing a pair of Beep arms (or flippers or flappers or whatever they're called).

"You don't need more Beeps, Beep. We're your family now," I said. "And to you we all say . . . yay!"

Everyone lifted their Beep arms. "YAY!"

Beep smiled, then grabbed me in a big hug.

"Who needs sweet," Lani said, "when we have Beep!"

I started to raise my hand, then lowered it when she shot me a look.

Because she was right. I may not have had any candy. But I had my good friends.

And so ended what really was the best Astroween ever.

SEND

Bob's Extra-Credit Fun Space Facts! (Even though nothing is fun about space!)

On **Earth**, every day is a **holiday** for someone somewhere! (Though they tell you about only some of them, so you don't get too many days off school.) Holidays usually come once a **year**, but here's the wild part: Since a year = the amount of time it takes for a **planet** to travel once around its **sun**, if you go to other planets, years are totally different lengths!

Like on **Mercury**, for example, one year = about 88 Earth days! Compare that to 365 and a quarter days for one Earth year, and think how rushed things must feel on Mercury. The baseball season probably has only about forty games (which is still *way* too many), and summer vacation must be over in a blink (though summer vacation *every*where is over in a blink).

On the other hand, since a **day** = the amount of time it takes for a planet to rotate one time on its **axis**, one day on Mercury = about 58 Earth days! Which means that if you ever moved to Mercury, you could probably pop a giant bowl of popcorn and spend an entire Saturday watching *all* the *Star Wars* movies in order, from *Episode IV* (IV is *Star Wars* for

"4 but really 1") to *Episode ZZZZZ* (which is *Star Wars* for "I fell asleep after they blew up the 600th Death Star").

Wait—does Mercury even *have* Saturdays?

TURN THE PAGE FOR A SNEAK PEEK AT THE

NEXT BEEP AND BOB ADVENTURE!

SPLOG ENTRY #1:
Hard Work Is Hard!

Dear Kids of the Past,

Hi. My name's Bob and I live and go to school in space. That's right, space. Pretty sporky, huh? I'm the new kid this year at Astro Elementary, the only school in orbit around one of the outer planets. There's just one micro little problem:

GETTING GOOD GRADES HERE IS NEARLY IMPOSSIBLE!

I mean, back on Earth at my old school, I got a

trophy for learning how to Velcro my shoe. But if you dare ask your teachers here for a little help putting on your space helmet the right way so your head doesn't explode, they deduct six points from your grade average and make you sharpen pencils for a week!

Beep just clapped and said, "Head go pop, yay!" Beep is a young alien who got separated from his 600 siblings when they were playing hide-and-seek in some asteroid field. Then he floated around space for a while, until he ended up here. Sad, huh?

You know what's even sadder? I was the one who found him knocking on our space station's air lock door and let him in. Now he thinks I'm his new mother!

On the bright side Beep not only likes sharpening pencils but also most of the other mind-numbing tasks I give him. Which frees up my time to do more important things like . . . like . . . like . . .

"Bob-mother like sleep late!" Beep said.

Well, who doesn't?

Beep is also really good at drawing, so I let him do all the pictures for these space logs (splogs as we call them) before sending them back in time for you to read. Beep says to tell you that he once was terrible at drawing, but that he worked really hard and that you can too. (Unlike me, of course, who was smart enough to give up art the second I realized I could draw only stick figures!)

Anyway, I promise to try to write more entries soon, maybe between my after-school nap and my predinner rest time.

Enjoy!

SPLOG ENTRY #2:
Sad and Sadder

Okay, so things didn't go exactly as planned. Somehow, I accidentally napped through dinner, and then I accidentally played video games for four hours, and now it's past midnight and I still haven't started my giant homework project that was assigned only two weeks ago and is suddenly due tomorrow.

Beep patted his tummy as he floated across the dorm room we share (sadly there's no gravity in space).

"Din-din yummy tonight," he said. "Beep eat for Beep and Beep eat for Bob-mother, too."

"Why didn't you wake me?"

"Bob-mother look cute when drool on pillow."

No one had ever called me cute before. But that was beside the point. "Listen, Beep, we have to focus on this project. Are you going to help me or what?"

Beep clapped. "Or what!"

"Help me look for the work sheet with the assignment written on it." I opened a drawer and a bunch of papers and junk floated out.

"This work sheet?" Beep said, holding up a floppy manila time-velope.

"No, that's for mailing our splog journals to the kids of the past."

Beep studied the time-velope. "Mail Beep and Bob-mother to past too?"

"We'd have to be two inches tall, Beep, to fit in

there. Besides, those aren't meant for mailing people."

Beep shoved the time-velope in his pouch. "This work sheet?" he said, holding up a crumpled paper.

"That's the one!" I grabbed it from him and read. "All we have to do is build an accurate model of a famous structure, such as the Eiffel Space Tower, using ice pop sticks."

Beep clapped again. "Ice pop sticks, yay!" Ice pops were kind of Beep's weakness.

"The best model in the class will be chosen to represent our school at the Ice Pop Stick Finals on Earth's moon. Which, you know, actually sounds kind of fun. I've never been to the moon."

"Beep neither."

I lowered the paper. "I've also never won anything. I wonder what that's like, to win a contest in front of everyone. With all the kids and teachers gazing up at you and everything. It must be the best feeling ever."

Beep clapped. "Bob-mother win prize! Go to moon!"

"Well, not *yet*. But I suppose there's a chance. If we work really hard."

"Bob-mother no like work hard."

"That is a problem." I straightened with resolve. "But you know what, Beep? We're going to do this project thing, and we're going to do it well. Okay, first we need about ten thousand ice pop sticks."

Beep raised his hand. "Oo, oo! Job for Beep! Job for Beep!" He spun. "Where ten thousand ice pop for Beep eat?"

"Sorry, Beep, that's not how it's done. Professor Zoome gave me *one* ice pop stick"—I reached into my backpack—"and this duplicator ray."

"Ray not look yummy."

"That's because it's a tool, not a treat. Watch." I let the ice pop stick float, aimed the duplicator, and pushed the button. A yellow ray zapped out. Suddenly, there were two floating sticks.

"See, Beep. Now we just have to do it"—I tried to subtract two from ten thousand in my head—"about ninety thousand and eight something more times." (I'm not so great at math.)

Beep folded his arms. "Beep like eat ice pop better."

"Well, we don't have ten thousand ice pops. So this will have to do." I handed the ray to Beep. "Here, you work on that while I start gluing the sticks together."

Beep immediately pointed the ray at my head. "Idea more better! Make two Bobs. Then work go two time fast!"

"No, Beep, wait—"

He pushed the button. *Click.*

Beep pouted. "No work."

"That's what I was trying to tell you. Duplicator rays are designed to work on objects only. Not life-forms."

"Bob life-form?"

"Yes, I'm a life-form!"

Beep pointed the ray at my desk. "Desk life-form?"

"No, but—"

Zap! Suddenly, there were two desks.

He pointed at the dresser. "That life-form?"

"Beep, we don't need another—"

Zap!

"Pillow life-form?" Beep said.

Zap! Zap! Zap!

"Stop that, Beep! This room is crowded enough!"

"Beep life-form?" He pointed at his foot.

Click.

His face grew sad when it didn't work. "But Beep want more Beeps."

"Sorry, Beep, that's not how it works."

He unscrewed a panel on the back of the duplicator

ray, exposing the wiring inside. "Beep have idea! Beep switch blue and red wire!"

I shot forward. "Beep, stop fiddling with that! You don't know how it works."

Beep put the panel back on. "Now Beep make ray work on life-form!"

"Give me that!" I said. But as I yanked it away, my finger may have brushed the button . . . just as the ray was pointed at Beep!

Zap!

"Oh no!" I froze. "What have I done?"

Beep looked down at himself and pouted. "Ray still not work on life-form. Beep sad."

Next to him, another Beep nodded. "Beep Two *sadder.*"

"Here tissue," the first Beep said, turning.

The second Beep dabbed his eyes.

And I promptly passed out.

SPLOG ENTRY #3:
Trouble Times Two

My eyes opened to the sight of Beep patting a wet cloth on my forehead.

"Thanks, Beep," I said. "For a second there I thought you had—"

A second Beep patted me with another wet cloth.

"Gaaahhhhh!" I said. "Beep, what have you done?!"

They looked at each other. Then the truth finally

hit them, and the two Beeps squealed, high-fived and hugged.

"Guys, keep it down!" I said just as there was a

knock on my dorm room door. It was followed by a voice: "Bob, are you okay in there?"

I pointed to the bunk bed. "Quick," I hissed at the Beeps. "Hide!"

Beep took his normal spot on top while, annoyingly, the duplicate Beep took *my* bed.

I opened the door a crack. "Oh, Lani, hey," I said.

Laniakea Supercluster is my best human friend at Astro Elementary. She's smart, cool, and fun, so I do my best to also act smart, cool, and fun whenever she's around. (The key word there is "act.")

"What's going on?" she said. "I was passing by and heard all this commotion."

"Oh, that was just Beep making some noise," I said. "And me. And Beep. I mean, Beep making more noise. *Not* a second Beep."

She gave me a funny look.

"So," I said, trying to change the subject, "what are you doing up so late?"

"Homework," she said.

"Me too!" I admitted. "After all, our ice pop stick thingies are due in just a few hours."

"Not *that* assignment, Bob. I finished that ages ago. I'm studying for my final exams for eighth grade."

"Eighth grade! But that's"—I counted on my fingers—"sixteen years from now!"

She laughed. "Not quite."

Beep and Beep giggled from the bed. I tried to talk loudly so she wouldn't hear them. "Speaking of science," I said, "I was wondering: What would happen if someone, uh, switched the red and blue wires on a duplicator ray and accidentally zapped their little buddy?"

Lani thought. "Theoretically, switching the wires could allow for animate organic matter, or *life-forms*, to be duplicated too. But as I said, only theoretically."

The Beeps gig-
gled again.

"So if someone
theoretically dupli-
cated someone," I
went on, "it would
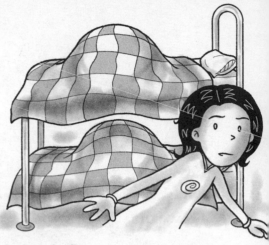
be pretty easy to reverse, right?"

She pinched her chin. "As far as I know, the cre-
ation of matter cannot be reversed without risking
total annihilation of the universe. Why do you ask?"

I gulped. "No reason. Well, nice talking to you.
Good night!"

I felt bad about closing the door on her, but I was
in a near panic. I shot around the room. "Quick,
Beep, I'll throw away the duplicator ray and you get
rid of the extra Beep."

The other Beep floated out from the sheets. "Get

rid of Beep Two make Beep Two sad." He flashed those big Beep eyes.

"Listen," I said, "I'm really sorry, but . . . would you stop looking at me like that?!"

"Bob-mother mean," Beep said.

Beep Two nodded. "We need new Bob-mother," he said, and promptly grabbed the duplicator from my hands.

I lunged forward. "NO, WAIT, I—"

Zap! A yellow flash blinded me. Then all I saw were blinking spots. But as those faded, a face came into focus. A face that looked exactly like mine.

"Hello, Bob," the other Bob said.

"Oh, hey," I answered back. And once again passed out.